Americano

Avocado
Baby

Persea gratissima

Avocado Baby

JOHN BURNINGHAM

Thomas Y. Crowell   New York

E

For Emms

Among other books by John Burningham

Borka (Winner of the 1964 Kate Greenaway Award)
ABC
Seasons
Mr Gumpy's Outing (Winner of the 1971 Kate Greenaway Award)
Mr Gumpy's Motor Car
Around the World in Eighty Days
Come Away from the Water Shirley
Time to Get Out of the Bath Shirley
Would You Rather . . .
The Shopping Basket

and the Little Books
The Baby The Blanket The Cupboard The Dog
The Friend The Rabbit The School

First published in Great Britain 1982
Copyright © 1982 by John Burningham
Jonathan Cape Ltd., 30 Bedford Square, London WC1

ISBN 0-690-04243-4 (tr)

ISBN 0-690-04244-2

LC 81-43844

Printed in Italy by New Interlitho, SpA, Milan
Phototypeset by Tradespools Ltd., Frome, Somerset

First U.S. Edition

Mr and Mrs Hargraves and their two children were not very strong. Mrs Hargraves was expecting another baby, and they all hoped it would not be as weak as they were.

The new baby was born and all the family were very pleased. Mr and Mrs Hargraves brought the baby home and it grew but, as they feared, it did not grow strong. Mrs Hargraves found feeding the baby very difficult. It did not like food or want to eat much.

"Whatever can I do," wailed Mrs Hargraves. "The baby doesn't like eating anything I make and it looks so weak."
"Why don't you give it that avocado pear?" said the children.

In the fruit bowl on the table there was
an avocado pear. Nobody knew how it had
got there because the Hargraves never
bought avocados. Mrs Hargraves cut the
pear in half, mashed it and gave it to
the baby, who ate it all up.
From that day on an amazing thing happened.
The baby became very strong.

It was getting so strong it could

break out from the straps
on its high chair,

pull other children uphill in a cart,

wrench off the side of its cot.
And each day Mrs Hargraves gave
the baby avocado pear.

One night a burglar got into the house.

The baby woke up and heard the burglar
moving about downstairs.
The baby picked up a broom,

and chased the burglar. The burglar was so frightened at being chased by a baby that he dropped his bag and ran out of the house.

The next day Mr Hargraves put a notice on the gate. "That should keep the burglars away," he said.

The baby would help
carry the shopping,
move the furniture
and push the car
when it would not start.

One day two bullies were waiting
for the children in the park.

The bullies started being very nasty to the children. The baby did not like that and jumped out of its push-chair,

picked up the bullies and

threw them into the pond.

The baby gets stronger every day and of course it is still eating avocado pears.

Persea gratissima